To my family, who taught me to find magic in the Australian bush from a young age.

First published in Australia in 2023 by Affirm Press,
a Simon & Schuster (Australia) Pty Limited company
Bunurong/Boon Wurrung Country
28 Thistlethwaite Street, South Melbourne VIC 3205
Affirm Press is located on the unceded land of the Bunurong/Boon Wurrung peoples of the Kulin Nation. Affirm Press pays respect to their Elders past and present.

New York Amsterdam/Antwerp London Toronto Sydney/Melbourne New Delhi
Visit our website at www.simonandschuster.com.au

11 12 10

A Cataloguing-in-Publication entry for this book is available from the National Library of Australia

A catalogue record for this book is available from the National Library of Australia

9781922930408 (hardback)

Cover and interior design by Brent Turner
Printed and bound in China by RR Donnelley Asia Printing Solutions Ltd.

WIRES is Australia's largest wildlife rescue organisation and has been rescuing and caring for sick, injured and orphaned native animals for over 35 years. WIRES's mission is to actively rehabilitate and preserve Australian wildlife and inspire others to do the same. Find out more at wires.org.au.

By purchasing this book you are supporting WIRES. Affirm Press donates 3% of gross profits and Brentos donates 3% of royalty earnings.

Acknowledgement of Country

Every animal, plant, stone, and star has a story to tell, and every page of this book was created on Traditional Country.

We acknowledge and honour the stories, the culture, and the history of First Nations people, who have always been, and always will be, the soulful custodians of these lands and seas.

Australia can feel like a magical land. Situated at the bottom of the planet, its unique animals enjoy a playground of incredible environments. From the Humpback Whale gliding through shimmering coral reefs, to the Bilby turning over the red soil of the desert, to the Black Cockatoo littering the ancient rainforest floor with eucalyptus seeds. This is a land where every living thing is connected and in tune with nature.

Let's take a journey to meet the curious animals that call Australia home.

As we journey from the beach to the bush, some animals are harder to find than others.

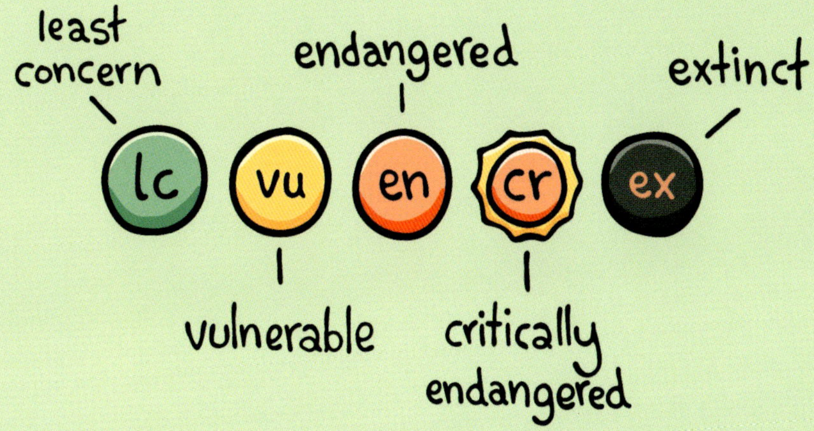

Some of these animals are not just hard to find in this book but are also hard to find in the wild.

Without our help they may face extinction.

Can you find them all?

Coral Reefs

Humpback Whale

least concern

lc

A Humpback Whale and her calf glide peacefully through the coral reef, which shimmers from the light of the morning sun.

Can you find...

Clownfish ×3

least concern

Bottlenose Dolphin ×3

least concern

Blue Groper ×2

least concern

Green Turtle ×6

least concern

Pygmy Seahorse ×1

least concern

Great White Shark ×1

vulnerable

Dugong ×1

vulnerable

Leatherback Turtle ×1

endangered

Australian Sea Lion

endangered

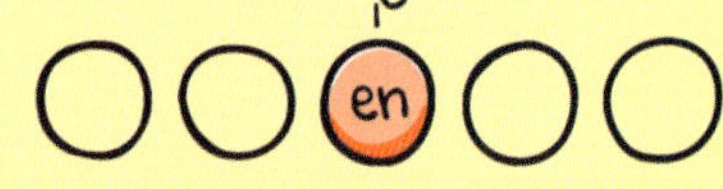

Australian Sea Lions hide in the depths of a vast underwater forest, seeking refuge from hungry predators.

Can you find...

Spotted Wobbegong

Blue-Ringed Octopus

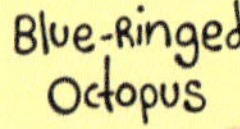

least concern

Leafy Sea Dragon

least concern

Giant Cuttlefish

least concern

Great White Shark

vulnerable

Loggerhead Turtle

endangered

Southern Right Whale

endangered

Southern Bluefin Tuna

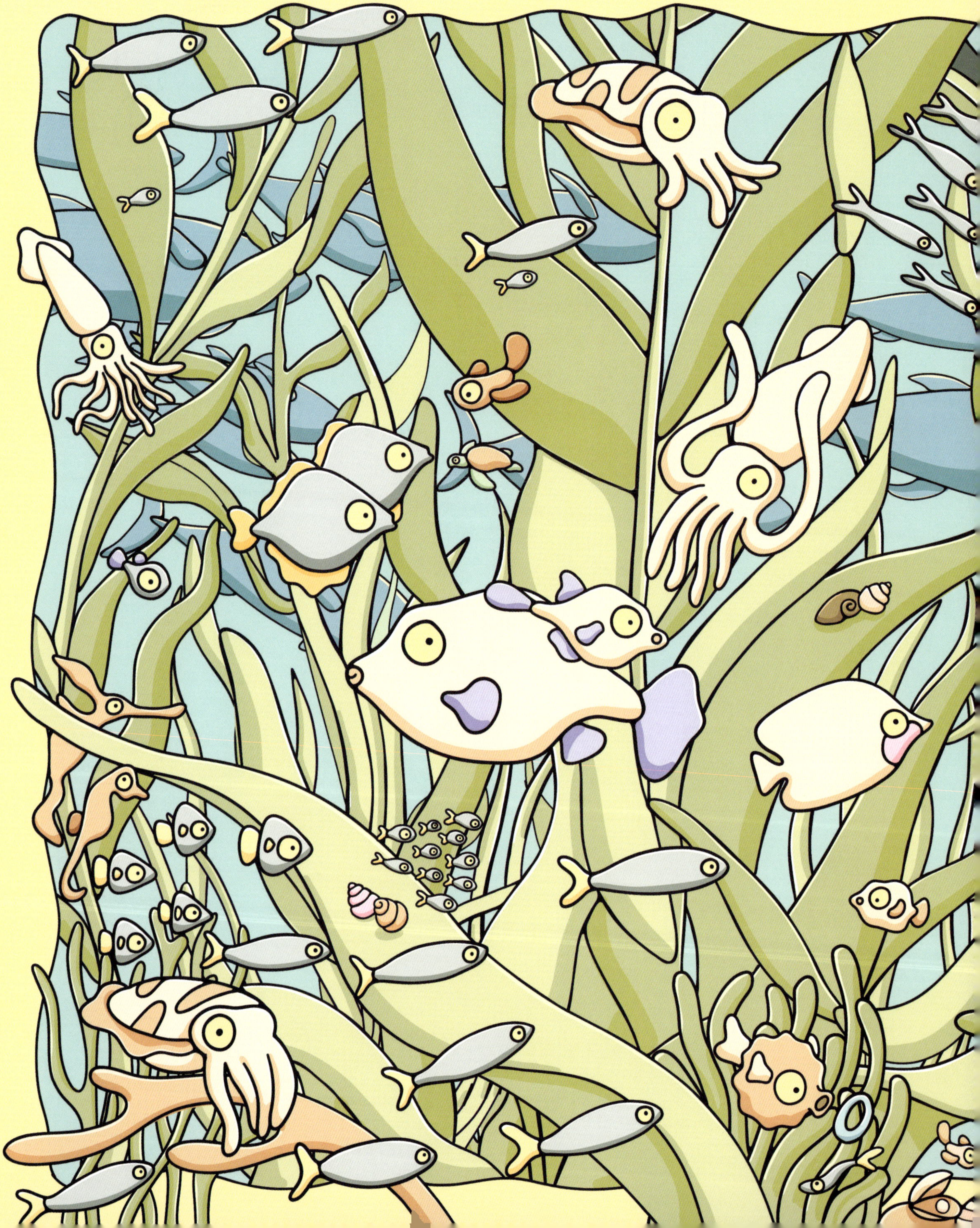

Kelp Forests

Loggerhead Turtle

endangered

en

Baby Loggerhead Turtles hatch from their eggs and make their way through powerful surf into the vast ocean.

Can you find...

Bottlenose Dolphin ×6

least concern

Silver Gull ×8

least concern

Leafy Sea Dragon ×1

least concern

Beaches
Minke Whale
×1
least concern
Swamp Wallaby
×2
least concern
Giant Cuttlefish
×1
least concern
Australian Fur Seal
×3
least concern
Short-Beaked Echidna
×1
least concern
Australian Little Penguin
×2
least concern
Koala
×3
endangered
Great Knot
×2
critical
Curlew Sandpiper
×2
critical

Coastal Forests

Koala

endangered

en

A Koala climbs to the top of the tallest tree in the forest while other creatures dart in and out of the tree hollows.

Can you find...

Laughing Kookaburra ×3 — least concern

Lace Monitor ×3 — least concern

Superb Lyrebird ×1 — least concern

Red-Bellied Black Snake ×1 — least concern

Dwarf Tree Frog ×5 — least concern

Greater Glider ×2 — endangered

Regent Honeyeater ×2 — critical

Leadbeater's Possum ×2 — critical

Red-Tailed Black Cockatoo

endangered

en

A pair of Red-Tailed Black Cockatoos perch regally on the branch of a river red gum in the warm sun.

Can you find...

Emu

×4

least concern

Tawny Frogmouth

×2

least concern

Tiger Snake

×1

least concern

Common Wallaroo

×3

least concern

Southern Hairy-Nosed Wombat

×2

vulnerable

Grey-Headed Flying Fox

×3

vulnerable

Southern Bent-Wing Bat

×1

critical

Helmeted Honeyeater

×3

critical

Rivers

Tropical Rainforests

Australian Cassowary

endangered

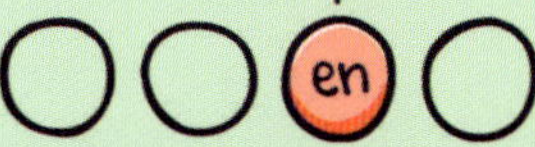

A powerful Australian Cassowary moves through the dense foliage of the forest floor, scanning for fallen fruit and insects.

Can you find...

Bennett's Tree Kangaroo

least concern

Platypus

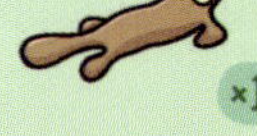

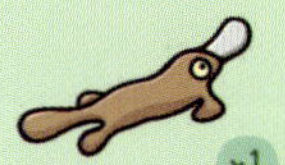

least concern

Saltwater Crocodile

×1

least concern

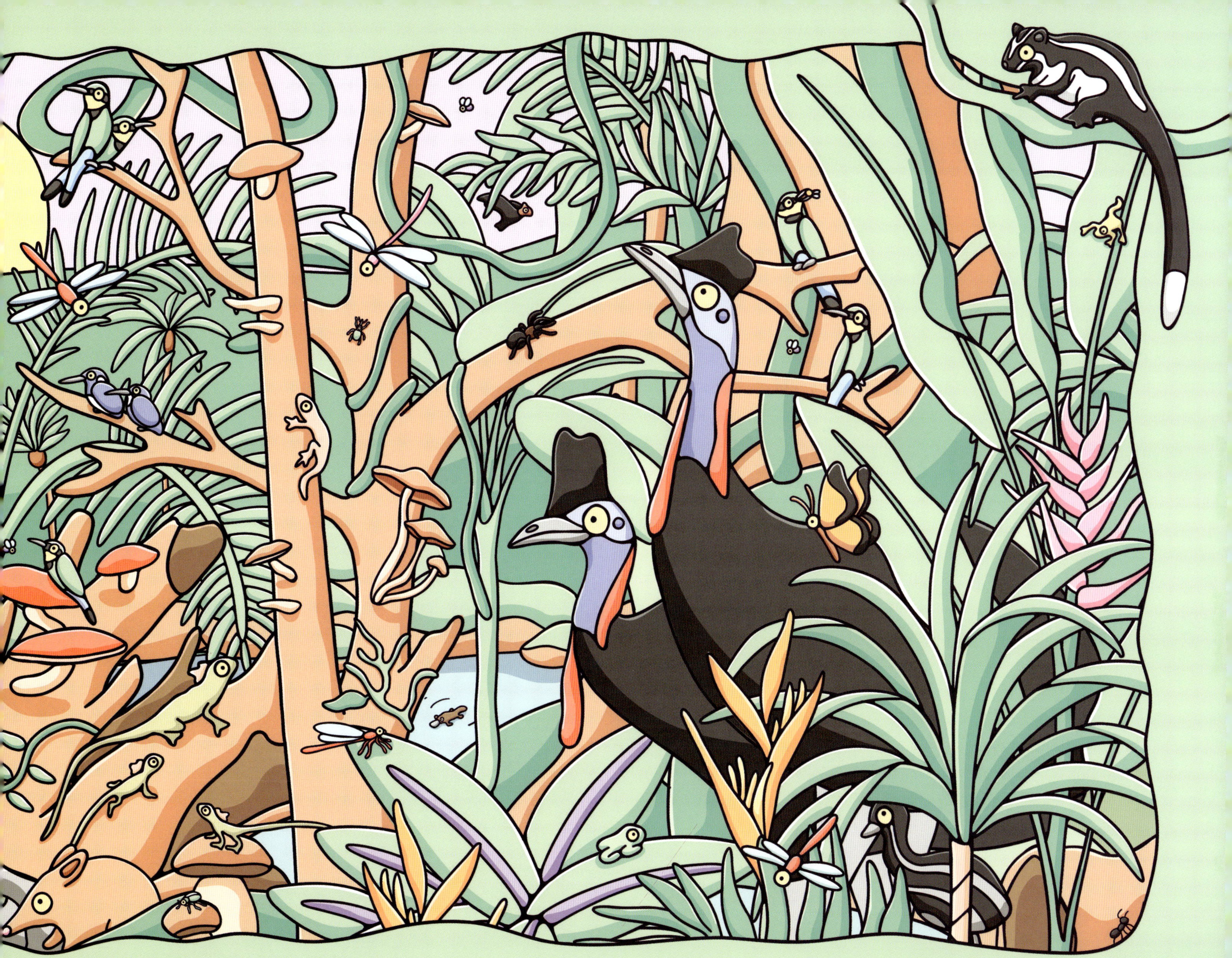

Rainbow Bee-Eater

×5

least concern

Striped Possum

×1

least concern

Squirrel Glider

×1

least concern

Green Tree Frog

×4

least concern

Short-Beaked Echidna

×2

least concern

Boyd's Forest Dragon

×3

least concern

Victoria's Riflebird

×2

endangered

Waterfall Frog

×4

endangered

Spectacled Flying Fox

×1

endangered

Mountains

Bare-Nosed Wombat

least concern

lc

A Bare-Nosed Wombat emerges from its burrow atop a high mountain peak to soak up the warmth of the midday sun.

Can you find...

Eastern Rosella

least concern

Short-Beaked Echidna

least concern

Eastern Grey Kangaroo

least concern

Emu

least concern

Yellow-Tailed Black Cockatoo

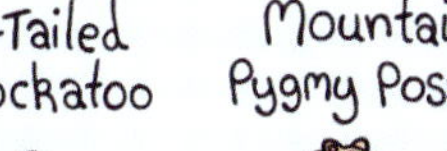

vulnerable

Mountain Pygmy Possum

endangered

Gang-Gang Cockatoo

endangered

Corroboree Frog

critical

Saltwater Crocodile

least concern

lc

A massive Saltwater Crocodile lurks in murky waters, waiting to snap its next meal.

Can you find...

Short-Eared Rock Wallaby

×3

least concern

Common Tree Snake

×1

least concern

Little Red Flying Fox

×4

least concern

Brolga

×7

least concern

Arnhem Land Gorges Skink

×1

endangered

Black-Footed Tree Rat

×1

endangered

Northern Quoll

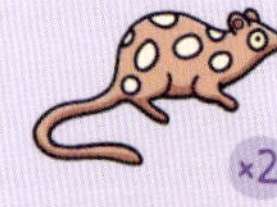

×2

endangered

Gouldian Finch

×4

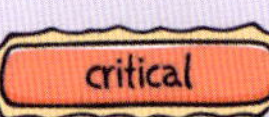

critical

Wetlands

Red Kangaroo

least concern

lc

A big Red Kangaroo bounds across the red desert under the blistering sun.

Can you find...

Emu

×7

least concern

Thorny Devil

×2

least concern

Stripe-Faced Dunnart

×2

least concern

Deserts

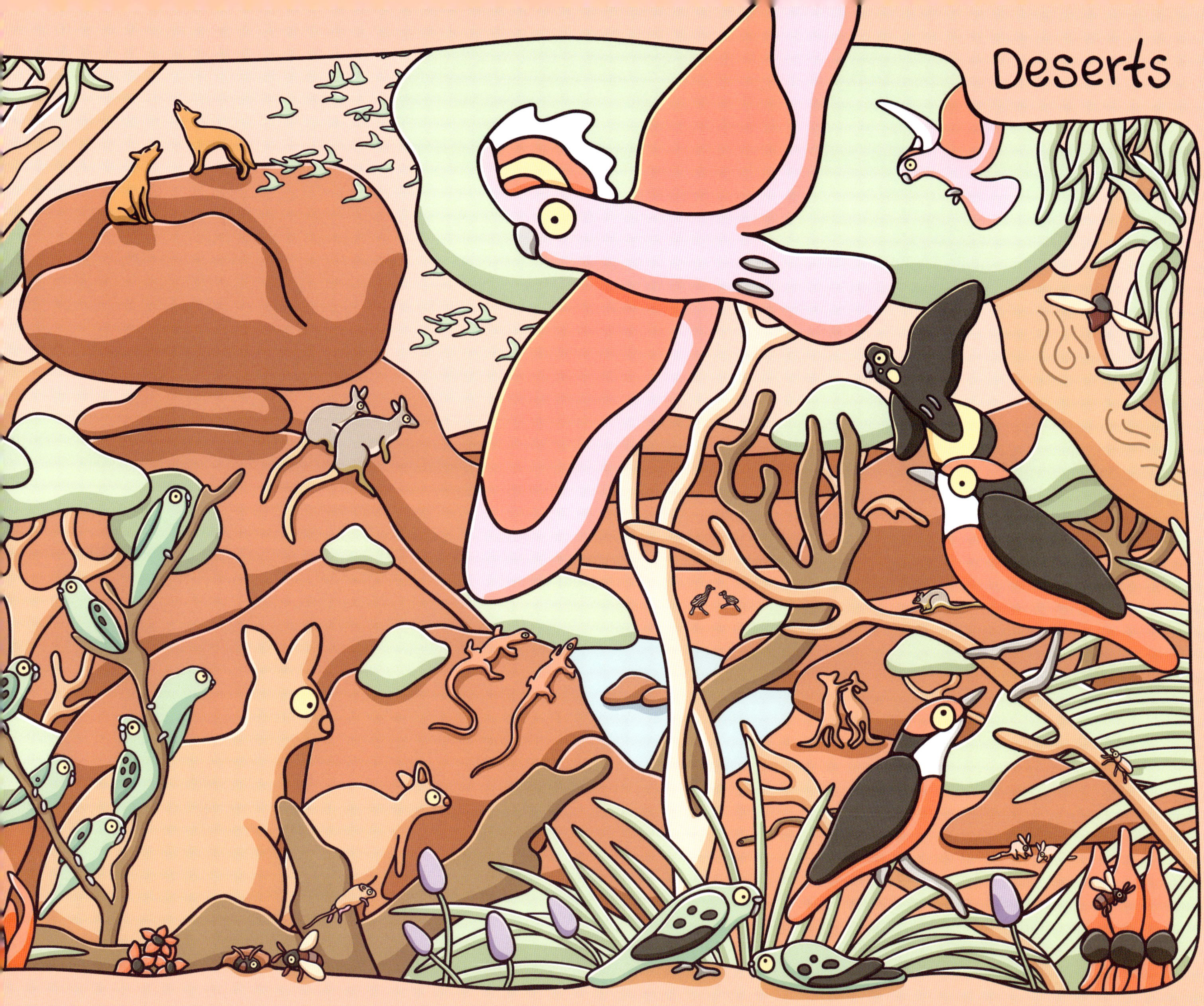

Dingo

least concern

Sand Goanna

least concern

King Brown Snake

least concern

Yellow-Footed Rock Wallaby

vulnerable

Dusky Hopping-Mouse

vulnerable

Kowari

vulnerable

Major Mitchell's Cockatoo

endangered

Night Parrot

endangered

Greater Bilby

endangered

Temperate Rainforests

Tasmanian Devil

endangered

en

A Tasmanian Devil scurries through the tangled undergrowth of an ancient forest.

Can you find...

- Platypus ×2 — least concern
- Moss Froglet ×9 — least concern
- Forester Kangaroo ×2 — least concern
- Bare-Nosed Wombat ×1 — least concern
- Gould's Wattled Bat ×3 — vulnerable
- Eastern Quoll ×1 — endangered
- Orange-Bellied Parrot ×6 — critical
- Swift Parrot ×7 — critical

Greater Bilby

endangered

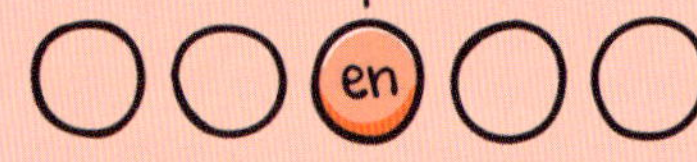

A Greater Bilby searches the wide open plains for insects to feed her joeys.

Can you find...

Frillneck Lizard

least concern

Northern Rosella

least concern

Short-Eared Rock Wallaby

least concern

Monjon

vulnerable

Death Adder

vulnerable

Goshawk

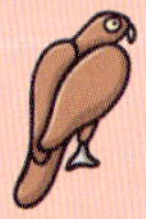

endangered

Northern Quoll

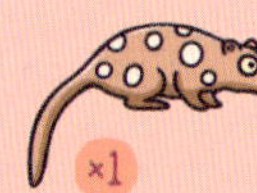

endangered

Purple-Crowned Fairy-Wren

endangered

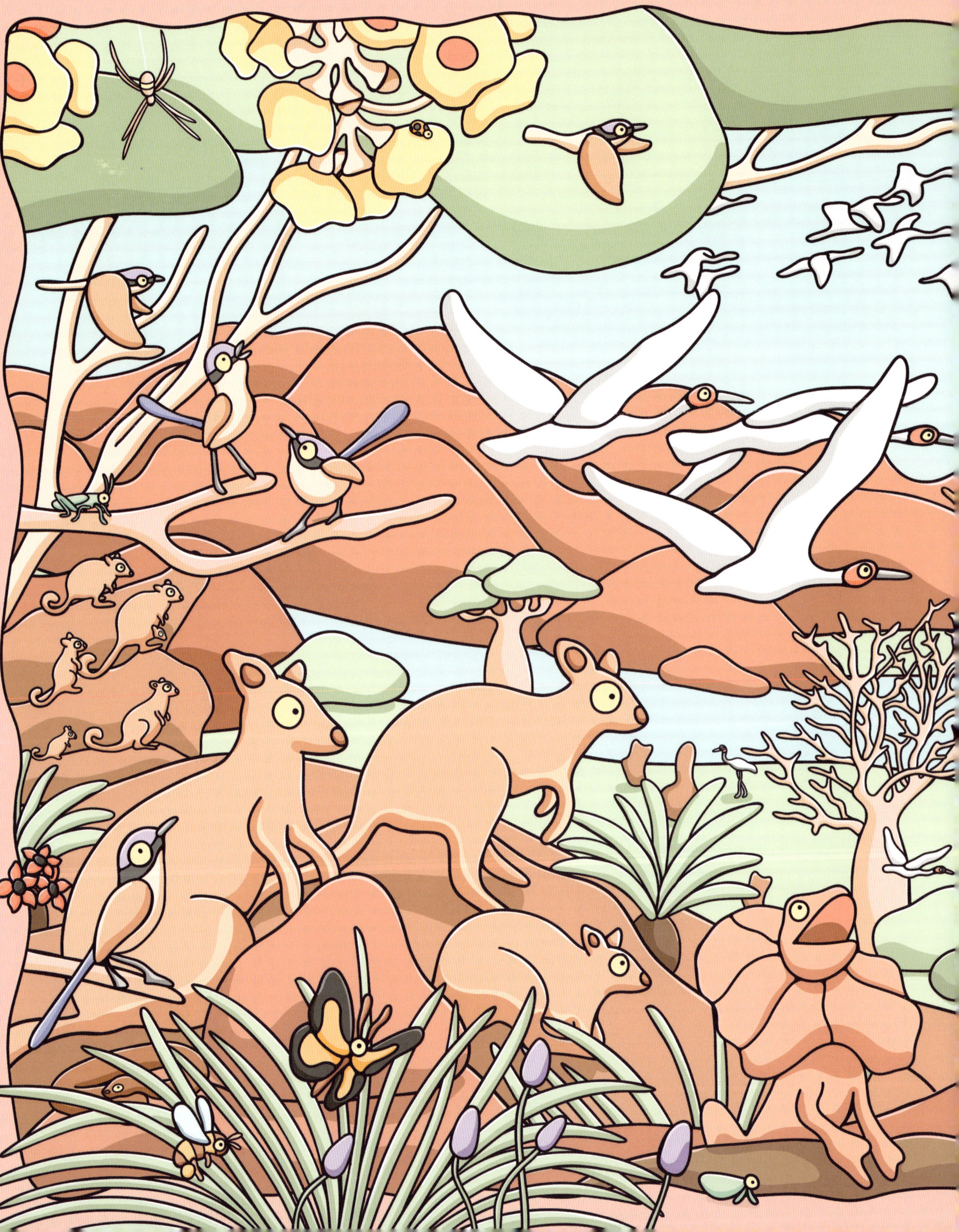

Savannas

Eucalyptus Forests

Quokka

endangered

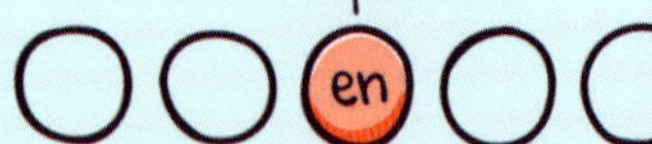

A family of Quokkas take shade under a majestic jarrah tree.

Can you find...

Tammar Wallaby

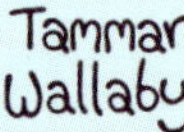

least concern

Honey Possum

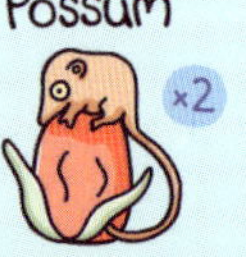

least concern

Western Rosella

x8

least concern

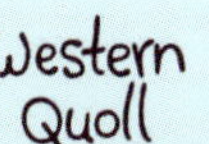

Western Quoll

×1

vulnerable

Sunset Frog

×4

vulnerable

Carnaby's Black Cockatoo

×8

endangered

Numbat

×2

endangered

Baudin's Black Cockatoo

×2

endangered

White-Bellied Frog

×1

critical

Western Ringtail Possum

×3

critical

Western Ground Parrot

×2

critical

Gilbert's Potoroo

×2

critical

Extinct Animals

extinct

    ex

Sadly, some animals that once roamed Australia's bushlands and beaches are now extinct.

Can you find...

Thylacine ×3

extinct

Lesser Bilby ×2

extinct

Tasmanian Emu ×3

extinct

Rusty Numbat ×1

extinct

Toolache Wallaby ×2

extinct

Paradise Parrot ×7

extinct

Short-Tailed Hopping Mouse ×1

extinct

Southern Gastric-Brooding Frog ×7

extinct

Many of Australia's vulnerable, endangered and critically endangered animals are nature's irreplaceable treasures. They each play a vital role in their habitats. By cherishing and protecting these extraordinary species, we not only preserve the beauty of nature that surrounds us but we also pass on a priceless gift to future generations, allowing them to experience the magic of these remarkable animals as we do today.

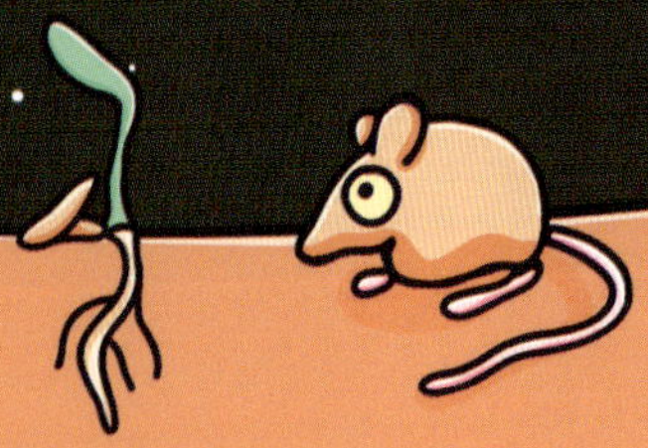

You can connect with nature and help Australian animals in small but meaningful ways. Here are some things you can do ...

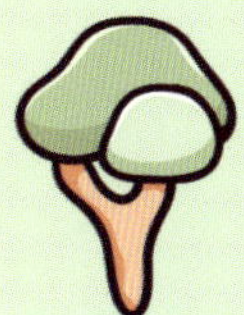

Plant native vegetation. Planting native trees and plants in your garden, school or local community spaces can provide food and shelter for native animals.

Create a wildlife-friendly garden. Provide water sources, nest boxes, and natural habitats for birds, insects and other native animals.

Remove litter. Pick up litter, especially plastic waste, to reduce the risk of harm to wildlife on land and in waterways.

Volunteer. Participate in local wildlife conservation groups or projects, such as tree planting, beach clean-ups, or animal surveys.

Learn and share knowledge. Educate yourself about Australian wildlife and their conservation needs, and encourage family and friends to learn more too.

Raise awareness. Place awareness posters around your neighbourhood to remind your community to look out for wildlife. Go to **brentos.com/raiseawareness** to get your free downloadable posters.

about the illustrator

Brentos grew up with the bush on his doorstep where he'd spend his free time exploring fire trails, building bush shacks and searching for yabbies in secret watering holes. If he wasn't in the bush, he'd be at the beach body surfing with mates or learning graphic design on his old computer.

From these early memories grew the inspiration for his work. His style is a nostalgic, cheeky type of pop art that hums with bubblegum pastels inspired by surf culture, subtle humour and the natural world.

He runs the Brentos art brand with his partner Tash. Together they paint murals, design surfboards and produce a range of merch, all with a mission to shine a gentle light on the beauty of Australian wildlife.

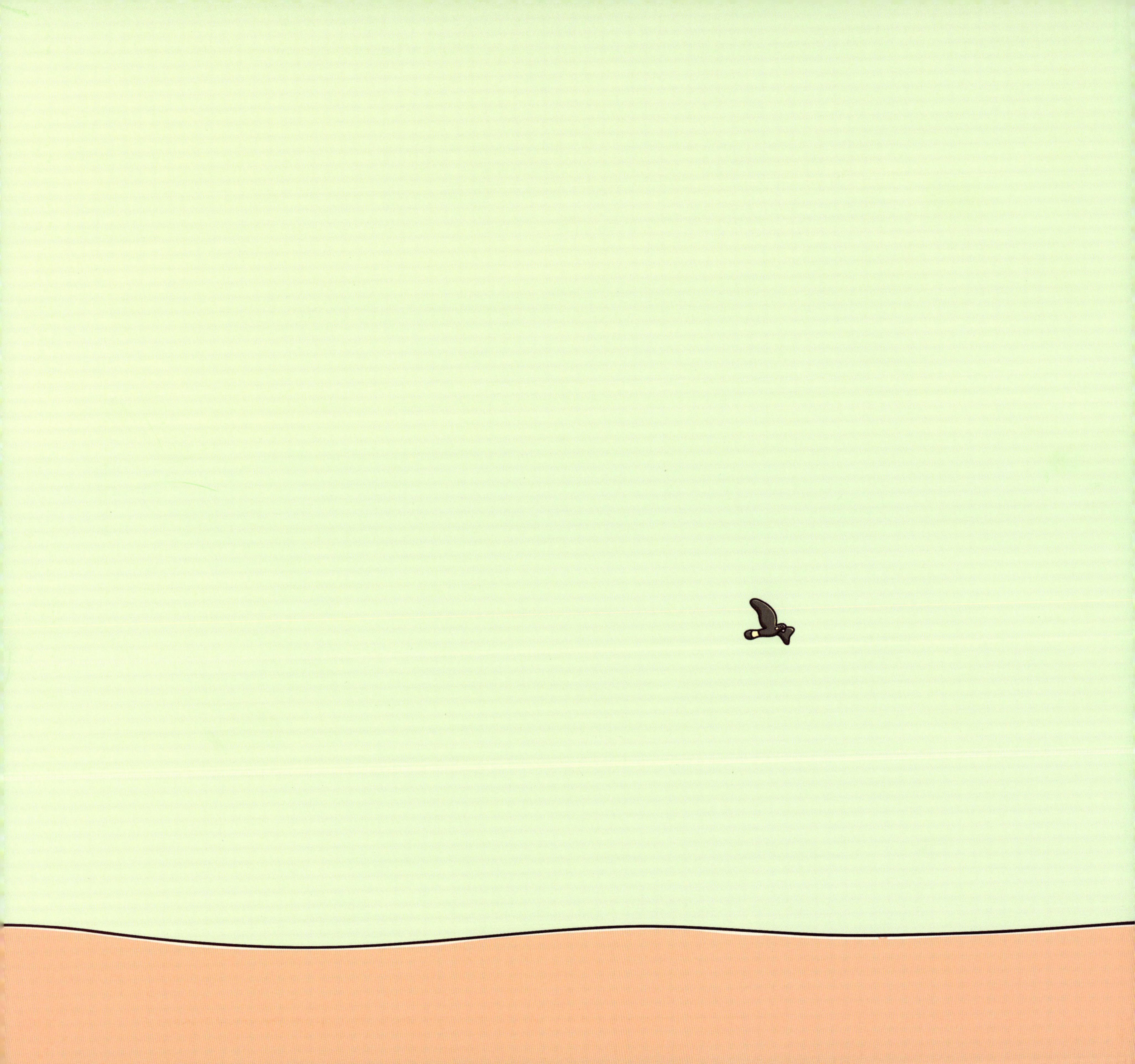